CRASH!

THE CAT

I'm
Krissie.

And I'm
Kait.

And this is . . .

I Like to Read® books, created by award-winning
picture book artists as well as talented newcomers,
instill confidence and the joy of reading in new readers.

We want to hear every new reader say, "I like to read!"

_____

Visit our website for flash cards, activities, and more about the series:
www.holidayhouse.com/ILiketoRead
#ILTR
This book has been tested by an educational expert
and determined to be a guided reading level G.

CRASH! THE CAT

David McPhail

I Like to Read®

HOLIDAY HOUSE • NEW YORK

To my Texas girls and their
wonderful cat, Crash, . . . with LOVE!

I LIKE TO READ is a registered trademark of Holiday House Publishing, Inc.

Copyright © 2016 by David McPhail

All Rights Reserved

HOLIDAY HOUSE is registered in the U.S. Patent and Trademark Office.

Printed and Bound in September 2017 at Tien Wah Press, Johor Bahru, Johor, Malaysia.

The artwork was created with pen, umber ink and watercolors.

www.holidayhouse.com

3 5 7 9 10 8 6 4 2

Library of Congress Cataloging-in-Publication Data

Names: McPhail, David, 1940- author, illustrator.
Title: Crash! the cat / David McPhail.
Description: First edition. | New York : Holiday House, [2016] | Summary:
"The family cat destroys everything in his path, and the two girls who
love him worry that he may be sick or blind in this story of unconditional
pet love"— Provided by publisher.
Identifiers: LCCN 2015045419 | ISBN 9780823436491 (hardcover)
Subjects: | CYAC: Cats—Fiction. | Pets—Fiction.
Classification: LCC PZ7.M478818 Cr 2016 | DDC [E]—dc23 LC record available at http://lccn.loc.gov/2015045419

ISBN 978-0-8234-3982-9 (paperback)

We call him Crash because
he crashes into things.

He crashed into Kait's drum.

And he crashed into Krissie's doll.

Here he comes.

CRASH!

Here he comes.

CRASH!

Uh-oh!

CRASH!

We were worried.
Maybe he was sick.
Maybe he needed glasses.

So we took Crash to the vet.

"He's fine,"
she said.

At home he crashed
into the clean clothes.

We had to wash them again.

Crash is a lot of work. But . . .
he lets us carry him.

And he lets us
dress him up.

And he always sleeps with us.

One night we heard a crash.

Where was our cat?

We all went downstairs.

Crash was
chasing a mouse.

The mouse ran into a boot.

So our father took
the little guy outside.

Life with Crash is always fun!